the HOSPITAL BOOK

by Lisa BROWN

CHILDREN'S HOSPITAL

EMERGENCY

NEAL PORTER BOOKS
HOLIDAY HOUSE / NEW YORK

Neal Porter Books

Text and illustrations copyright © 2023 by Lisa Brown
All Rights Reserved
HOLIDAY HOUSE is registered in the U.S. Patent and Trademark Office.
Printed and bound in October 2022 at C&C Offset, Shenzhen, China.
The artwork for this book was created using India ink and watercolor on paper.
www.holidayhouse.com
First Edition
1 3 5 7 9 10 8 6 4 2
Library of Congress Cataloging-in-Publication Data is available.

ISBN: 978-0-8234-4665-0 (hardcover)

When I went to the hospital, I cried nine times.

The first time I cried was when my stomach hurt.

The second time I cried was
when the car went over a bump.
It made my stomach hurt more.

The third time I cried
was in the waiting room.

There were other kids there, too.
Some of them were sick.
Some of them were hurt.
Some of them played games
or watched screens or fought
with their sisters and brothers.

A lot of them cried.

I didn't cry when the nurse took my temperature.
Or measured my blood pressure.

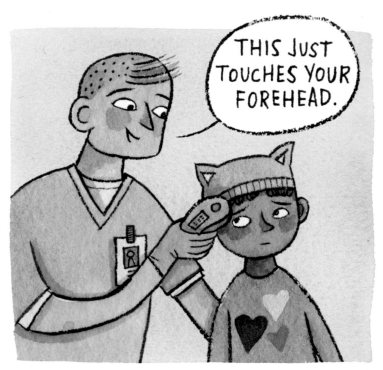

Or figured out how much oxygen I had in my body.

I didn't cry when I got a bracelet with my name on it.

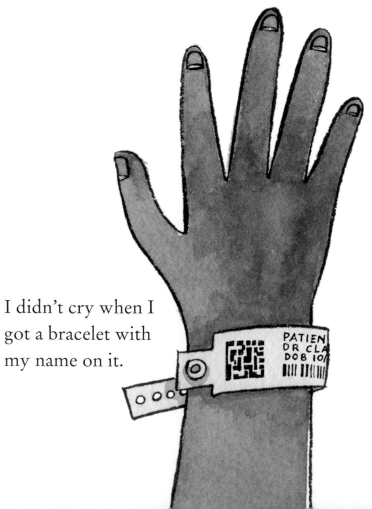

The fourth time I cried was when a doctor pressed on my stomach with her hand and asked if it hurt.

It did.

I didn't cry when I got a funny robe with ties in the back.

I didn't cry when I got new socks with dots on the bottoms.

I almost cried when I had to take off my favorite hat, but I didn't.

So that doesn't count.

The fifth time I cried was because of a needle. Even though the nurse put cream on my arm so it wouldn't hurt.

IT'S JUST A TINY POKE!

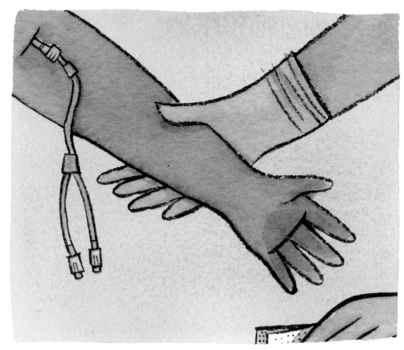

First the needle took some blood out of my arm. Then it made room for a tube.
It was still scary. But it didn't hurt.

IT'S CALLED AN **IV**. MEDICINES AND LIQUIDS GO THROUGH THE LITTLE TUBE.

THE SLEEVE HOLDS THE IV IN PLACE.

CAN I GET JUICE IN IT?

SNIFF

I got a sticker because I was brave.
I was brave even though I cried.

SNIFF

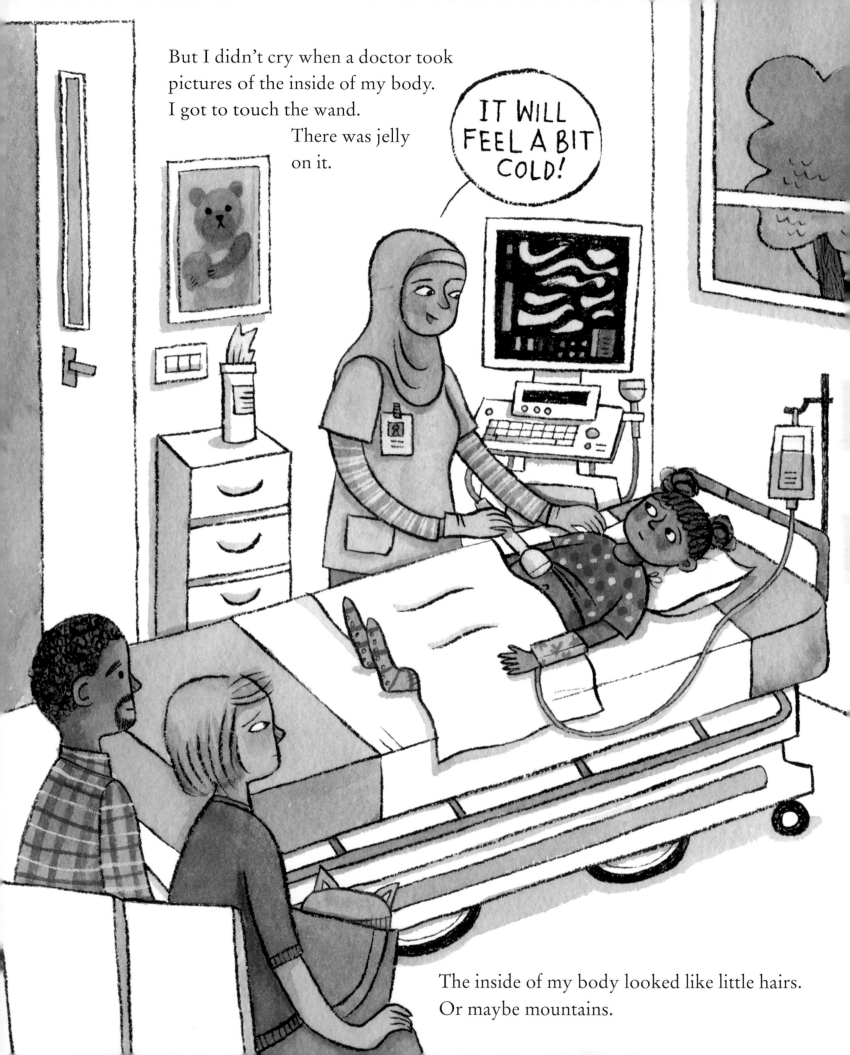

But I didn't cry when a doctor took pictures of the inside of my body. I got to touch the wand. There was jelly on it.

IT WILL FEEL A BIT COLD!

The inside of my body looked like little hairs. Or maybe mountains.

I didn't cry when the doctor said that I needed an operation.
But then I saw my mom and dad crying a little bit.

So I cried a little bit, too.

ELEMENTARY

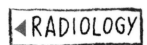

AS I SUSPECTED, SHE HAS APPENDICITIS! BUT IT'LL BE OKAY NOW THAT WE CAUGHT IT.

YOU'LL FEEL MUCH BETTER VERY, VERY SOON!

But that doesn't count.

The sixth time I cried was when an orderly pushed my bed down the hall.

It was a little scary, but also a little fun.

The seventh time I cried was when I was in the operating room. I was scared of all the people in masks.

I was scared when it was time to wear my own mask.

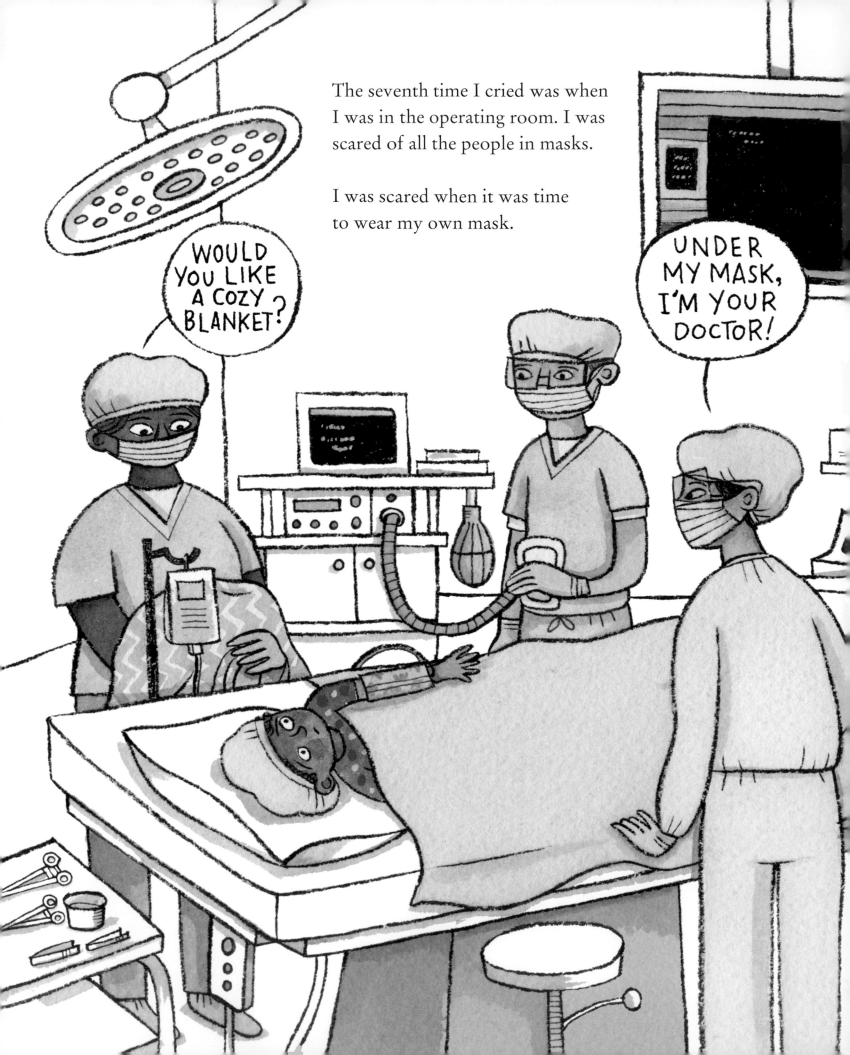

I'LL BE HERE UNTIL YOU FALL ASLEEP!

9
8
7

The doctor counted backwards.

6
5

4
3
2

She said I'd be asleep by the time she got to **1.**

I didn't believe her.

1

Because I wasn't tired.

I didn't cry when I woke up.

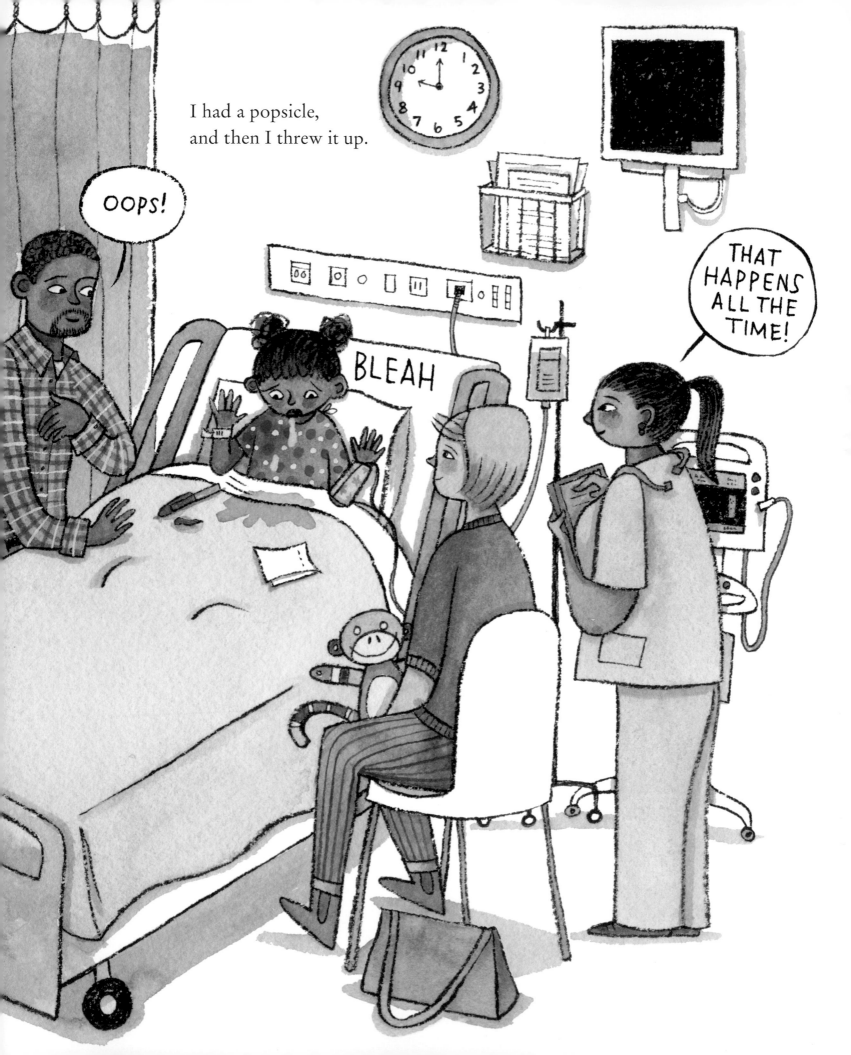

The eighth time I cried was when it was nighttime. I cried because my new room was filled with beeping machines. I cried because it smelled funny. I cried because nurses kept coming in to check on me.

The ninth time I cried
was because I was lonely.

Even though I wasn't alone.

In the morning, I didn't cry. Even when the pancakes didn't have blueberries inside.
I like pancakes best when there are blueberries inside and strawberries on top.

I didn't cry when I walked around the hallway.

Even when my balloon popped.

I didn't cry when I met a dog. It licked my face.

I didn't cry when I rode in a wheelchair. It squeaked.

When I got home from the hospital,
my stomach didn't hurt anymore.

I wasn't scared.
I wasn't lonely.

I got to wear my own pajamas
and my favorite hat and keep
the bracelet with my name on it.

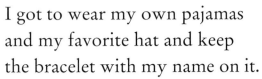

And my grandpa cried
and my auntie cried
and my brother cried
and my friend cried

and my mom and dad cried
and I cried, but also we
were all smiling,

so that doesn't count.

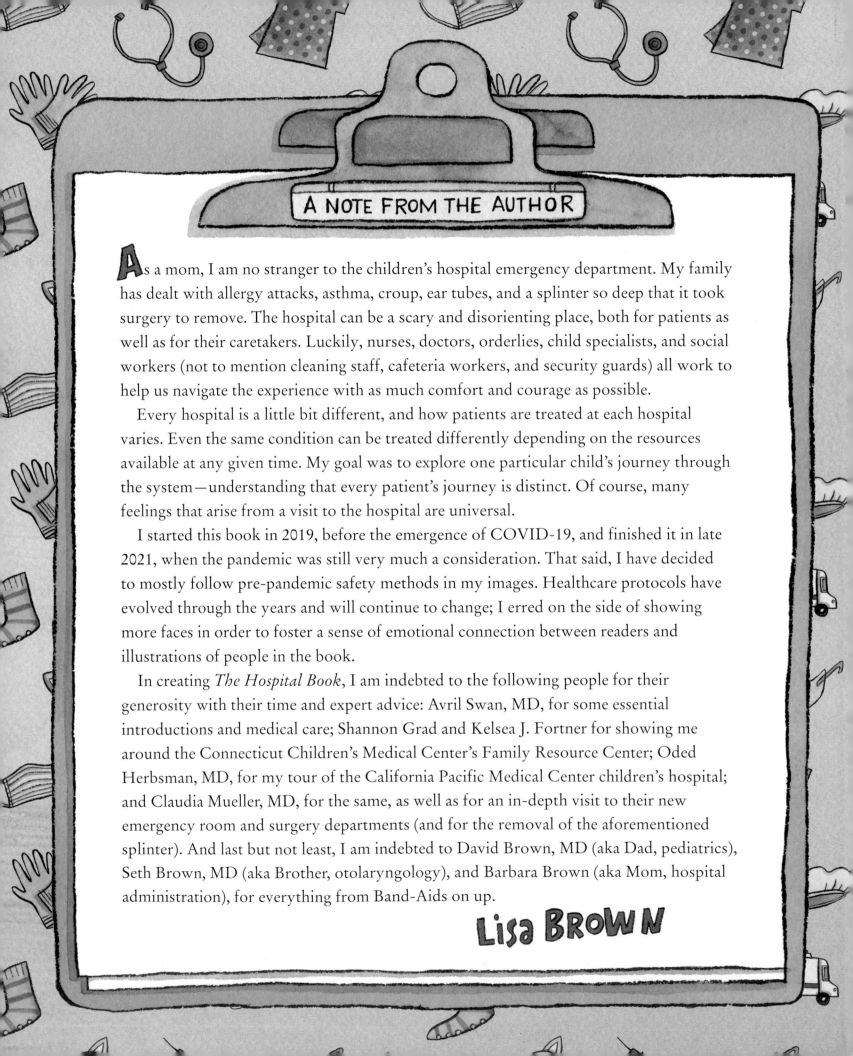

A NOTE FROM THE AUTHOR

As a mom, I am no stranger to the children's hospital emergency department. My family has dealt with allergy attacks, asthma, croup, ear tubes, and a splinter so deep that it took surgery to remove. The hospital can be a scary and disorienting place, both for patients as well as for their caretakers. Luckily, nurses, doctors, orderlies, child specialists, and social workers (not to mention cleaning staff, cafeteria workers, and security guards) all work to help us navigate the experience with as much comfort and courage as possible.

Every hospital is a little bit different, and how patients are treated at each hospital varies. Even the same condition can be treated differently depending on the resources available at any given time. My goal was to explore one particular child's journey through the system—understanding that every patient's journey is distinct. Of course, many feelings that arise from a visit to the hospital are universal.

I started this book in 2019, before the emergence of COVID-19, and finished it in late 2021, when the pandemic was still very much a consideration. That said, I have decided to mostly follow pre-pandemic safety methods in my images. Healthcare protocols have evolved through the years and will continue to change; I erred on the side of showing more faces in order to foster a sense of emotional connection between readers and illustrations of people in the book.

In creating *The Hospital Book*, I am indebted to the following people for their generosity with their time and expert advice: Avril Swan, MD, for some essential introductions and medical care; Shannon Grad and Kelsea J. Fortner for showing me around the Connecticut Children's Medical Center's Family Resource Center; Oded Herbsman, MD, for my tour of the California Pacific Medical Center children's hospital; and Claudia Mueller, MD, for the same, as well as for an in-depth visit to their new emergency room and surgery departments (and for the removal of the aforementioned splinter). And last but not least, I am indebted to David Brown, MD (aka Dad, pediatrics), Seth Brown, MD (aka Brother, otolaryngology), and Barbara Brown (aka Mom, hospital administration), for everything from Band-Aids on up.

Lisa BROWN